THE TURNAROUND

MASON FALLS MYSTERIES
THE TURNAROUND

R. T. MARTIN

darbycreek

MINNEAPOLIS

Darby Creek
A division of Lerner Publishing Group, Inc.
241 First Avenue North
Minneapolis, MN 55401 USA

For reading levels and more information, look up this title at
www.lernerbooks.com.

Cover and interior images: iStock.com/two3design (baseball); AlenKadr/Shutterstock
.com (texture); iStock.com/Vectorfactory (skyline); iStock.com/nuiiun (baseball field).

Main body text set in Janson Text LT Std 12/17.5.
Typeface provided by Adobe Systems.

Library of Congress Cataloging-in-Publication Data

Names: Martin, R. T., 1988– author.
Title: The turnaround / R.T. Martin.
Description: Minneapolis : Darby Creek, [2018] | Series: The Mason Falls mysteries
    | Summary: When the struggling Mason High Lions baseball team suddenly starts
    winning after many disappointing seasons, Avery and his friend Katie investigate
    whether someone is cheating.
Identifiers: LCCN 2017018576 (print) | LCCN 2017036380 (ebook) |
    ISBN 9781541501201 (eb pdf) | ISBN 9781541501119 (lb : alk. paper) |
    ISBN 9781541501195 (pb : alk. paper)
Subjects: | CYAC: Baseball—Fiction. | Cheating—Fiction. | Friendship—Fiction. |
    High schools—Fiction. | Schools—Fiction. | Mystery and detective stories.
Classification: LCC PZ7.1.M37346 (ebook) | LCC PZ7.1.M37346 Tur 2018 (print) |
    DDC [Fic]—dc23

LC record available at https://lccn.loc.gov/2017018576

Manufactured in the United States of America
1-43783-33635-8/17/2017

CHAPTER 1

"The Rays lost again. That can't be a good omen," Justin said, looking at the sports news on his phone.

"What else is new?" Katie replied sarcastically, without looking up from the doodle she was making in her math notebook. "If you care about winning, you should switch your allegiance to a different minor league team. And probably a different high school team too."

Justin shot a glance at Bryce, who sat next to Katie and across from Justin at their usual lunch table. After all, Bryce was the shortstop on their high school baseball team. But he didn't look offended by Katie's remark. He took a bite

1

of his hot dog and spoke with his mouth full. "Nobody's going to be disappointed in *our* team this season."

Katie looked up from her notebook. "Didn't you tell me that you guys only won two games last year?" Katie had moved to Mason Falls at the beginning of the school year. Her locker happened to be next to Justin's, and as soon as Justin discovered that she liked baseball, he'd known they were destined to be friends. But Katie didn't share his long history of loving the Mason Falls Lions.

She was right about this, though—the team had performed terribly in the previous season. "But a lot of the games we lost were really close!" Justin insisted.

"And that was last year," Bryce said confidently. "We still had Mr. Bartlett as our coach then. He was on the verge of retirement and didn't really care about the team anymore. He actually fell asleep for an entire inning once. This year we have Coach Savino."

"Oh yeah, the new geography teacher, right?"

"I thought it was geometry," said Justin.

Bryce shrugged. "Whatever. Coaching baseball is the main reason he's here. The guy used to play for a minor league team. He almost played in the *majors*. He's making a huge difference for us. Plus, we've got Derrick."

Justin saw Katie was about to ask another question. "Derrick Ellis," Justin told her. "He just transferred here. He's a pretty strong batter—at least according to his stats."

Katie rolled her eyes. "Of course you already looked up his stats. Nerd."

Justin grinned and shrugged. He'd been a baseball nerd for as long as he could remember, and he was proud of it. When he was younger, he'd played little league—until the bike accident. His left knee had popped out of its socket and never healed properly. Now he was highly prone to dislocating that knee, which prevented him from trying out for baseball— or any other sport for that matter. Instead, he became the ultimate fan. He didn't get to see much live baseball, though. Occasionally, he and his dad would drive to see the Rays, a minor league team not far away, but that only happened two or three times a year. So he was always excited for the first game at his high school.

"I'm just saying," Justin told Katie, "if he can nail a couple of home runs, Derrick could really help turn things around."

"See?" Bryce said. "He gets it. With Derrick and Coach Savino, this could be the year we win state."

Katie sighed. "How many people are on a baseball team?"

"On ours? Seventeen," he said. "If you include the coach, eighteen."

"So two people account for one-ninth of the team. I know that because I've been doing *this*." She tapped her pencil on her math notebook with a smile. "That's a small percentage. How much of a difference can two people make?"

"When one of them is the coach, a lot," Bryce said.

"I'll believe it when I see it."

"Can't your glass be a little more half-full?" Justin said.

"It is half-full," she said. "It's half-filled with a terrible team."

The bell rang, signaling the end of lunch. "Good luck tonight," Justin said to Bryce as the three friends stood up to leave the cafeteria. Bryce, still chewing, gave a little wave as he headed off to class.

"I take it you're going to the game?" Katie asked.

"Yup, always do," said Justin. He was used to going to Lions games alone, but this year Katie had promised to come too.

"I'll pick you up at six thirty."

"Why do you even want to go if you think the team's going to lose?" He kept the question light, but he was genuinely curious how she'd respond. She didn't have his years of Lions loyalty, and he didn't want her to be bored or depressed by a bad game.

"Because I want to support my friends," Katie laughed. "I went to your debate thing too. That wasn't exactly a thrill ride. I don't even remember who won."

"They did," Justin said, smiling.

Justin and Katie had study hall this period, so they headed into the library and took a table by a window. Katie opened her math textbook, and Justin pulled out the book they were reading in English. He read a couple paragraphs but was distracted thinking about Katie's pessimistic attitude.

"Coach Savino is going to make a difference this year," he said. "Also, a good batter can make a *huge* difference."

She rolled her eyes and went back to her homework.

Justin went back to reading, still thinking about what Bryce had said. *This could be the year we win state.*

CHAPTER 2

There weren't many fans at the game that night. The team's terrible record had caused dwindling attendance over the last few years. Most of the people in the bleachers were players' family members. When Justin and Katie arrived, Justin headed straight for the top of the bleachers. "Why do we always have to sit in the back?" Katie asked.

"You have the best view of the entire field when you're back here," Justin said, settling into his spot. It wasn't just the field that Justin wanted to see. From their vantage point, they could even see into the dugouts. A lot of other schools' dugouts had roofs over them, but

Mason Falls High School hadn't bothered to spend much money on the baseball team's facilities. "There's Coach Savino." He pointed to a man in a windbreaker and a hat, both with the team's logo on them. He was talking to some of the players in the dugout while others warmed up.

"Where's this new batter?"

Justin scanned the players. He knew all their numbers as well as their names. "He's over there."

Derrick was by the dugout near home plate. He was holding two of the team's wooden bats and practicing his swing—something Justin had only seen pros do.

"I don't know," Katie said. "He doesn't look like much. Hey, why does our team have wooden bats? My last school had metal ones."

Justin shook his head. "Our school won't buy metal bats. Apparently, you have to win games to get a budget."

"So we're already at a disadvantage?"

"What did I say about your glass being half-full?"

"Like I said, it is half-full, but part of it is filled with inferior bats."

Justin rolled his eyes.

Bryce was warming up near third base. He caught sight of his friends and gave a little wave. Katie waved back, and Justin gave him a thumbs-up. As Bryce went back to warming up, Katie said, "Oh, hey, Matt Spencer's here."

Justin's attention snapped back to the bleachers. Matt was sitting a couple rows in front of Justin and Katie. Last year, Matt had been the second baseman. But he'd been kicked off the team halfway through the season, and no one, including Bryce, knew why. Mr. Bartlett, the old coach, had kept that information to himself, and Matt hadn't been close with anyone on the team, so nobody had heard the full story from him. In fact, Justin wasn't sure Matt had friends at all.

Justin looked over at Katie. "You know Matt?"

"Yeah, we had woodshop together last semester." Katie raised her voice. "Hey, Matt!"

He turned around but just barely. As Katie waved, Matt gave her an uncomfortable nod and then returned to staring at the field.

Katie let her hand drop. "As you can see, we're best friends," she said.

Justin chuckled a little. "Don't take it personally. He's always been like that."

Before long the game started. The away team, the Spartans, would bat first. The Lions pitcher, a guy named Kyle, took the mound, and Justin leaned forward, watching closely. Kyle held the ball behind his back, waiting for a sign that would tell him what kind of pitch to throw. Justin glanced over at the Lions' dugout, where Coach Savino stood. Mr. Bartlett's signs had always been painfully obvious. He'd pull on his hat brim to signal a fastball, tap his left shoulder for a changeup. Anybody who was paying any attention could've figured out the pattern within an inning or two. Opposing team members had often picked up on Mr. Bartlett's signs and anticipated the Lions' next moves—it had been pretty embarrassing. Justin hoped Coach Savino would take a different approach.

Savino made an elaborate gesture—clearly a decoy sign meant to throw off the other team. Justin figured the real sign was buried somewhere in that confusing flurry of motion. *Smart*, he thought. *The guy does know what he's doing.*

The catcher saw the sign. Justin knew he'd make his own gesture, hidden by his legs and his glove, for only the pitcher to see. Kyle, standing on the mound, saw the catcher's sign and nodded. In one fluid motion, he wound up and whipped the ball right over the center of the plate. The batter didn't have a chance—it was too fast. The impressive first pitch even caused the few fans to give a collective "Ohhh" and applaud briefly.

"Wow," Katie said. "Good start."

"See," Justin replied, "this is going to be our year."

Last year, Kyle had given a mediocre performance, but he was doing significantly better this game. He struck out two batters, throwing six strikes and only two balls. The third batter hit the first pitch, but it was a pop-fly almost straight up. The catcher caught it with barely any effort. The crowd clapped and whistled as the Lions stepped up to bat.

Justin leaned forward, tense with excitement. "Here we go."

Derrick was up first. He stepped into the box, tapped the bat on the plate and got into a ready stance for the pitch. The pitcher got the signal from the catcher, nodded, wound up, and threw the ball.

CRACK.

Derrick connected perfectly. Justin knew what would happen. *That one's out of here*, he thought. Sure enough, the ball flew over the outfield fence.

The crowd gave a standing ovation as Derrick rounded the bases, pumping his fist in the air. He got encouraging pats on the back from Coach Savino and the rest of the team as he went back into the dugout.

"Okay," Katie said. "Maybe you guys were right."

"I've never seen a ball go *that* far in a high school game," Justin murmured.

"What?" Katie said. "You sound suspicious."

Justin ran some numbers in his head. He was trying to figure out how far the ball would have flown in an actual stadium. He figured it would have gone deep into left field, possibly hitting the outer wall if it had been able to roll instead of landing in the tall grass.

"Well, don't get me wrong, I'm happy. It's just—that's *really* far."

"Especially using a wooden bat, right?" Katie added.

"Yeah," Justin said. "I didn't even think of that."

"Maybe he's just that good."

"I guess," Justin said, trying to shake off the suspicion.

At the end of the inning, the Lions were up one to zero. Kyle pitched another good inning. Two Spartans players managed to get on base, but neither made it home before Kyle pitched three strikes for the third out. When the Lions were up to bat, they only got one guy to first base. This was more like what Justin was used to seeing from them. But in the third inning the Lions surged ahead with two RBIs, making the score three to zero.

As he watched the third inning, that sneaking suspicion came back to Justin. Derrick had smashed the ball out of the park, but it wasn't just him. All the players seemed to be hitting significantly better than they had last year. The Lions typically hadn't been strong hitters, and Justin always blamed it on their lack of metal bats. This season, that seemed to be changing. Justin tried to shrug off the feeling. The change was probably just the result of good coaching.

/////

The score was eight to two at the end of the game, and the Spartans had only narrowly gotten those two runs.

The small crowd went crazy after the last out, but something still didn't sit right with Justin. He clapped for his team, but without a smile. And he noticed that one person wasn't standing for the victory. Matt was seated, quickly tapping something into his phone.

Maybe he's jealous, Justin thought. *The team just got a big win without him.*

"Come on," Katie said, pulling him out of his train of thought. "Let's go see Bryce."

They headed down to the fence behind their team's dugout. Players were high-fiving and patting each other on the back in celebration. Bryce spotted his friends approaching, came out of the dugout, and made his way over to the fence.

"Great game!" Katie said, hanging on to the chain link and talking to Bryce through it.

Bryce grinned. "I told you things were going to be different this year."

"Coach Savino must be pretty pleased," said Justin.

"He's thrilled!" Bryce said. "He's buying us pizza."

Justin tried to keep his voice casual. "Do you think he'd mind if I talked to him? I'm curious about his coaching style."

Justin figured Bryce wouldn't see anything strange in that, since he knew how much Justin loved to talk strategy. "Go ahead. He's over by the cooler."

Justin walked around the fence and found the coach sitting on a bench looking at his phone. "Hi, I'm Justin Avery. That was a great game."

Coach Savino looked up and nodded briefly. "My players did a great job."

"Yeah, especially at bat. I've never seen any high school player hit a ball as far as Derrick did. Have you been focusing a lot on batting?"

"I focus on everything. Every aspect of the game is important, and any player can be great if they're taught correctly." Coach Savino stood up, sliding his phone into his pocket. "Nice meeting you, uhh—"

"Justin," he said again.

"Right, Justin. I've got some things I have to take care of, but thanks for coming out tonight."

"I'll be at every game," he said, but the coach was already walking away.

Justin was about to return to his friends when he saw Derrick packing some stuff into a bag. He walked over. "Hey, you're Derrick, right?"

"That's right," he said without looking up.

"I'm Justin Avery, longtime Lions fan. You're probably the best hitter this team has ever had."

"I know." He still didn't even look up.

"If you keep slamming balls like that, you're on track to be the next Edgar Martínez."

Derrick looked up at Justin. "Who?"

Justin was shocked the guy didn't know who he was talking about. "Edgar Martínez. You know, he was a major league player." Derrick was still looking at him blankly. "He's one of the best designated hitters of all time."

Derrick scoffed. "Well, I'm going to be *the* best designated hitter of all time, no question."

Justin raised his eyebrows. "Uhh, okay."

"Listen, kid," Derrick said.

"I think we're the same age," Justin interjected, but Derrick kept speaking as if he hadn't heard.

"I've got a lot of people who want to congratulate me, so I can't really talk now."

Justin looked around and saw no one standing behind him waiting to talk to Derrick.

"Ooookay," Justin said. "Well, it was—uhh—nice to meet you." Derrick just picked up his bag and walked away.

During the ride home in Katie's car, Justin was still distracted. Eventually, Katie noticed that he was being quieter than usual and asked, "What's going on with you?"

"I'm not sure," he said, "but I'm going to find out."

CHAPTER 3

"So you think they're cheating?" Katie asked Justin as she stuffed books into her locker the next morning.

Justin glanced around to make sure no one was listening to their conversation. Other students chatted at their lockers and rushed through the hall on their way to class. Nobody seemed to be paying attention to Justin and Katie. Still, he kept his voice low. "I'm not saying that, but it *is* strange that they're doing so well so suddenly. The whole game just felt off to me."

Katie cocked an eyebrow. "What happened to a couple of new players making such a big difference?"

"Hey, guys!" Bryce had come up behind Justin. "What's up?"

"Not much," Katie said lightly. "We were just talking about the game last night. You guys really hit it out of the park, pun intended."

Bryce smiled proudly. "I'm telling you, this is going to be the year we win state." All three of them started walking down the hallway toward their first class of the day. "Coach Savino's been working us really hard, but it's worth it if we can keep playing like that."

"What have you guys been working on in practice?" Justin asked.

"Fundamentals over and over and over again, but it's really helping. Plus, Coach has all this insider baseball knowledge that's really helpful."

"Insider knowledge?" Katie said.

"Yeah," Bryce said excitedly. "Tricks he learned when he was in the minor leagues. Little stuff you wouldn't normally think about, like using certain bats during practice and keeping other bats for games. That way, the game bats are in the best condition for games

and not all beat up from getting used every
day. Plus, the heavier bats help with our swing.
Coach said wooden bats can actually be an
advantage if you know what you're doing."

"Huh," Justin said. All of that made sense.

"And I guess you believe me about Derrick
now, right? Guy's unbelievable," Bryce added.

Good choice of words, thought Justin.

"Yeahhhhh . . ."

Bryce shot him a sympathetic look. "You
talked to him, didn't you?"

Justin nodded.

"Yeah, he's a little hard to take, but if you
could do what he can, you'd be like that too."

"Would I, though?" Justin said skeptically.

"Well, you know what I mean."

They walked past a few rooms in silence
until Justin couldn't keep his thoughts to
himself any longer. "Actually, I looked up
Derrick's stats again last night. His record
at his old school is solid, for sure, but it's
not *amazing*."

"A player's only as good as his coach,"
Bryce said.

"So . . . nothing seems weird to you at all?"

Bryce looked confused now. "What do you mean?"

Katie said, "I think what Justin is trying to say is that the team got really good really fast. Has anything else changed? Anything else that contributed to such a huge turnaround?"

Bryce stopped in his tracks.

"Wait. You think we cheated somehow?" He looked as if Katie had just punched him in the gut, and it made Justin feel awful. He didn't want to doubt his friend's success, but he couldn't deny that the game had felt weighted in the Lions' favor.

"We don't think *you* cheated," Justin assured him quickly. "But the team made such a turnaround so fast that it seems like—it seems like maybe it's more than just Coach Savino and Derrick that made the difference."

"I can't believe this." Bryce threw his hands in the air. "We finally win a game, and my two best friends think the only way we could have done it was by cheating."

"Bryce—" Justin started, but Bryce cut him off.

"I guarantee you no one on this team is using any kind of sketchy performance-enhancing pills or anything . . ."

"I never said you were," said Justin.

"Then what do you think we're doing? How do you think we're cheating?"

"I don't know!" Justin burst out. "I'm sorry I even brought it up! Forget I said anything, okay?"

Bryce scowled at him for a moment, then sighed and shook his head. "Whatever, man. Just—look, don't bother coming to the rest of the games if you think we're just cheating our way through them. I don't want you there if you're not there to support us."

"Of course he's there to support you," said Katie, sounding slightly annoyed. "Why else would he be there?"

"It's called living through others," Bryce muttered, so quietly that Justin wasn't sure he heard him right. More loudly, he said, "Look, it's fine. I'll see you guys later."

Bryce stormed off down the hallway, leaving Justin and Katie behind him.

"That went well," Katie said as they started walking again.

"He's right, though," Justin said. "It's not fair of us to accuse anyone of cheating unless we have evidence."

Katie's eyes glinted in a way that Justin recognized. This was the look that meant *challenge accepted.* "Okay then," she said. "I guess we'll have to find some evidence."

CHAPTER 4

The next two days were a mix of good news and bad news. The good news was that Bryce really did seem to forget about that uncomfortable conversation. He acted normal around Justin and Katie, except that they all avoided talking about baseball.

The bad news was that Justin and Katie had no luck gathering evidence—or any information at all. Justin, who was friendly with several other Lions players, made a point of catching up with them. But when he asked about the team, they only told him the same things Bryce had said: Coach Savino, Derrick, big difference this year, could win state, the end. Meanwhile Katie researched various cheating methods online. But she told Justin that nothing jumped out at her as a plausible explanation for the Lions' turnaround. Everything that happened in the major leagues seemed too elaborate, too expensive, or both.

"The stats really do seem suspicious, though," Justin said to Katie as they sat in a booth at the pizza place near the school. Justin had downloaded spreadsheets of the Lions players' records onto his phone. He summed up his main takeaways for Katie.

"Nine players had a significantly better performance in this first game than they had all season last year. Last season, Bradley Nachov only got three runs. In this week's game, he got a run and a triple. Doug Pocar couldn't hit it out of the infield last year, and he got two doubles!"

"Aren't we forgetting someone?" Katie asked. "What about Coach Savino? What if he's helping the team cheat?"

Justin shook his head. "He's obviously been working the team really hard to prepare for each game. If he were cheating, I think he'd be a little more lax about practice."

"But he'd gain a lot from the team doing well. His coaching record would be better, and he'd have job security."

"But the school didn't get rid of the last coach even though we had the worst record of any team in the state. There's no reason for him to cheat. He could even get fired for it."

Katie shrugged. "Fair enough."

"The only people who stand to gain from the team doing well are the players," Justin said. "A lot of them want to get college scholarships. Maybe even get into the minor leagues, like Savino did. The stronger their record, the better chance they have."

Katie nodded thoughtfully. "But if they're doping, they could get in serious trouble."

"I don't think anyone is doping. They can get randomly drug tested at any time, and I doubt they'd take that kind of risk."

"And I don't know how else they could be cheating. Which brings us back to square one."

The more he thought about it, the more Justin began to believe that he had just been imagining things. Maybe Coach Savino had really kicked the team into gear, and the addition of Derrick inspired all the other players to do a little better. Maybe they were just sick of losing.

There could be a lot of explanations that didn't involve cheating.

/////

When Katie picked him up to go to the second game of the season, Justin was almost ready to let the issue go entirely.

"I had a new idea for our investigation," she said the moment he got in the car.

Justin shrugged. "I've kind of let that go. We shouldn't be accusing the team of cheating anyway."

"You wouldn't be saying that if you had talked to Matt," she said as she backed out of the driveway.

"Matt Spencer? The disgraced former second baseman?"

"What makes you think he's disgraced?"

"Well, he got kicked off the team in the middle of the season last year. That wouldn't have happened unless he did something to deserve it. Especially back when Mr. Bartlett was in charge." The previous coach hadn't exactly been known for being tough on his players.

"Well, if you don't know the details you shouldn't assume anything," said Katie reasonably. "Anyway, I happened to run into Matt coming out of woodshop yesterday."

"I didn't think you had woodshop this semester."

"I don't, but Ms. Hernandez sticks around after school and lets anyone who's taken her class use her equipment. It's an informal thing she does. I'm working on this little statue of a lizard monster . . ."

"And the point of this story is?"

"That I talked to Matt about the team."

"How is that helpful? Matt's not even *on* the team anymore."

"He may not be on the team, but he definitely knows something."

"What makes you say that?"

"Remember after the last game, he didn't stand up and applaud like everyone else?"

"You noticed that too?"

Katie rolled her eyes. "I see everything, Justin. Instead of clapping, he was typing on his phone." She turned the radio down a little. "I think he was taking notes. Maybe he'd been looking for something specific during the game and then wrote it down afterward."

"So . . . you think he's looking for cheating too?"

"Right. When I talked to him, I got the sense that he's still pretty mad about getting kicked off the team. If he catches someone cheating, it'd be the perfect revenge."

"Okay . . . ," said Justin. "But did he actually tell you he suspects anyone?"

They stopped at a light, and Katie looked over at him. "Not exactly. But I did mention what an amazing batter Derrick is, and he said—and I quote: 'Yeah. Believe me, I've noticed.' He said it in a really low, dramatic voice too."

"So let me get this straight," Justin said. "You think that Derrick's cheating, and Matt's trying to catch him to get back at the baseball team for kicking him off?"

"Correct." The light turned green and Katie started driving again. "So I think we should try to team up with him. If we work together we might have a better chance of figuring out what's going on. Because I really do think your instincts were right, Justin. *Something* is going on."

/////

The game was at a different school about thirty minutes away. When he and Katie arrived, Justin headed for the back row of the visiting team's bleachers. On their way, they passed Matt, who was also sitting near the back. Justin nodded to him and Katie gave him a little wave, but he just looked down at his phone, ignoring them.

"Yeah, he really seems like prime sidekick material," Justin said sarcastically as they took their seats.

"Maybe if you acted a little friendlier . . . ," Katie said with a shrug. "Besides, this isn't the best place for us to say 'Hey, do you think the team is cheating? Us too!' Let's find him at school tomorrow. He might be less standoffish if we talk to him in private."

There were more Lions fans in the stands for this game. It still wasn't crowded by any stretch of the imagination, but especially for an away game, this was a decent turnout. Word must have gotten around that the team was doing better this year.

The Lions were up to bat first. Derrick took the plate, tapped his wooden bat on it twice, and got into a proper stance.

The pitcher leaned in, staring hard at the catcher, then nodded and stood up to throw. He wound up and threw a curve ball. Derrick swung.

"Strike!" the umpire shouted.

The ball flew back to the pitcher. This time, he threw a fastball, but Derrick didn't swing.

"Strike!"

The third pitch was a ball that nearly hit the dirt, but the fourth sailed right over the plate, and just like in the previous game, Derrick nailed it. It flew high over center field and past the fence—another home run. The designated hitter rounded the bases, pumping his fist in the air—apparently his signature move—while the fans in the visitors' bleachers applauded.

It was the only point the Lions scored that inning, and during the second one, the opposing team tied it up. By the fifth inning, the score was three to two, but by the seventh, it was six to three in the Lions' favor. A few times, Justin glanced over at Matt, who was hunched forward and watching intently, his hands fidgeting restlessly.

The Lions got three runs in the eighth inning, allowing only one run to be scored against them, and they managed to shut out the opposing team in the ninth. The final score was nine to four. The Lions had won again.

When the game was over, Justin saw Matt hastily type something into his phone, then get up and leave the bleachers. Justin and Katie strolled down to their team's dugout. While Katie and Bryce talked, Justin sidled over to the team's bench, where Derrick was sitting. "Good game," Justin said.

"Thanks," Derrick replied in between gulps of his sports drink.

"You've hit two home runs in your first at bat in two games. That's pretty impressive."

"I'm pretty good," he said flatly.

"You weren't doing this well last year, though, right? And your previous school probably had metal bats. What's different here?"

"Coach Savino." Derrick jerked a thumb toward the new coach, who was sitting at the other end of the dugout talking to some other players. "He's the best coach I've ever had."

Justin cocked an eyebrow. "How so?"

"The guy knows what he's talking about. Like with the bats, yeah, most other schools have metal ones, but Coach Savino knows that you can swing a wooden bat harder and faster than a metal one. You just have to adjust your stance a little." He finished the last of his drink.

"Huh," Justin said, "I didn't know that."

"Yup. But I'm not supposed to talk strategy with anybody. Not even fans. So keep that to yourself." Derrick stood up and tossed the empty bottle into a trashcan.

Justin took that as his cue to leave. He gave Derrick a nod that the designated hitter didn't return. Then he walked down the bench to the new coach. "Great game, Coach!"

"Thanks." He looked up from his phone and squinted at Justin. "You were at the last game."

"Justin," he said, hoping the third time would be the charm when it came to introducing himself. "Derrick says you're the best coach he's ever had."

"Wouldn't know," Coach Savino said, slipping his phone into his pocket. "I never met his other coaches."

"He said that you think wooden bats are sort of an advantage."

"If you swing 'em right." He still wasn't looking at Justin.

"So you've seen that kind of power hitting with wooden bats before? Derrick's not super unusual for a high school player?"

"Every player is unique."

That wasn't an answer, but Justin could see that this was a pattern with the new coach.

"Well, I just wanted to say congrats on turning the team around. It's nice to see them win for a change."

/////

As he and Katie headed to her car, Justin recapped his conversations with Derrick and Coach Savino.

Katie jangled her car keys in one hand, thinking. "You know what?" she said after a moment. "It's the bats. It's got to be."

"What do you mean?"

"The way Derrick focused on the wooden bats . . . it reminded me of something. When I was researching cheating methods online, I saw a lot of stuff about cheating in the major leagues. Tampering with bats."

"What kind of tampering?" Justin asked as they got into Katie's car.

"Corking, for example. You hollow out the middle of the bat and fill it with a lighter material, usually cork, but it can be done with rubber too."

"Sure, I've heard of that," said Justin. "If the inside of the bat is lighter, you can get a more powerful swing, right? That would explain why average hitters on the team have been crushing it."

Katie nodded and started the engine. "And why Derrick is hitting more home runs than he did at his old school."

Justin frowned. "But I've never heard of a high school team doing that to their bats."

"Neither have I." Katie peeled out of the parking lot a little faster than necessary.

"That's why it didn't occur to me as a possibility till now. But you know why it's probably not a problem in high schools? Because most high schools have metal bats."

Justin drew in his breath. "You're right," he said. "Or at least that's a good theory. But how do we prove it?"

"Let's start by talking to Matt. Maybe he can help us get to the bottom of this."

CHAPTER 5

After school the next day, while Bryce was at baseball practice, Justin and Katie headed to the woodshop. "Excuse me, Ms. Hernandez, do you know where I could find Matt?" Katie asked the woodshop teacher.

"Oh, he doesn't come here on Fridays," Ms. Hernandez replied.

"Yeah," added one of the students in the room. "On Fridays he usually heads to the library for an hour or so to do homework."

Katie thanked the teacher and steered Justin back into the hallway. "Sounds like a depressing Friday afternoon for Matt," Justin murmured as they headed for the library.

"I mean, look how we're spending our Friday afternoon," Katie pointed out.

"Investigating possible cheating is way more exciting than doing homework!"

"That's the spirit," Katie said approvingly.

Matt was at a table in the corner. He was nose-deep in an assignment when Justin and Katie approached him.

"How's it going, Matt?" Katie said.

He looked up from his papers. "Oh, you know. Just trying to pass history class."

Justin wasn't sure how to respond to that, so he just launched into what he'd planned to say. "Great game last night, right?"

Matt's face was expressionless. "Yeah, they did really well."

"It's pretty mind-boggling, considering that the team did so horribly last year."

Matt leaned back in his chair and crossed his arms. "I know what you're trying to say."

Justin waited.

"You're saying that the team is doing better because I'm not on it anymore."

That surprised Justin. "What? No—that's

not what I was trying to say at all."

"We just saw you at the game and thought you might want to talk about it," added Katie hastily.

"Oh," Matt said and uncrossed his arms. "Sorry, some of the guys on the team have been saying that's part of why they're doing better." He looked back at his assignment.

Justin felt awkward standing next to the table, so he sat down across from Matt. Katie took the chair next to his. "I actually thought you were pretty good when you were playing. I go to all the games. I don't think you were a weak link—I think they're doing better because of Derrick."

"Yeah, Derrick," Matt said as if he didn't believe it or simply didn't care. He looked back down at his work, ducking his head.

"I thought you agreed that Derrick was worth keeping an eye on," said Katie neutrally.

Matt kept his eyes on the papers in front of him. "Oh, he is."

This must be what Katie had been talking about before—Justin was definitely getting the sense that Matt wasn't telling them something. "We noticed you were paying really close attention to the game. I'm curious what your take was."

Matt looked up. "Well, I noticed some general things. A few outfielders were out of position. Some of the batters"—he smirked at Justin—"including your friend, Bryce, had poor stances when batting. Things like that."

Justin glanced over at Katie. She jumped in: "We've been noticing some stuff too. Not exactly that kind of stuff, but—maybe something a little shadier. Does that interest you at all?"

Matt's face instantly changed. It went from bored to something closer to angry. "No," he said forcefully. "That doesn't sound like something I'm interested in. And if you don't mind, I'm trying to focus on my homework right now."

It was clear Matt wasn't going to give up whatever he knew. "Ah," Justin said, getting out of his seat, "fair enough. See you at the next game, I guess?"

"Wouldn't miss it," Matt said grimly.

Katie gave Matt a little wave and then followed Justin out of the library. "I don't get it," Justin said to her, shaking his head. "If his goal is the same as ours, why doesn't he want to team up with us?"

"We're Bryce's friends," Katie pointed out. "Bryce loves the Lions—and so do you. Maybe Matt doesn't trust us. He might think that even if we do find evidence of cheating, we won't report it, or we'd stop him from reporting it."

"Well, anyway, I guess we're on our own," Justin sighed.

"So how do we find out if someone's messed with the bats?"

Justin didn't like what he was about to suggest. Somehow, it felt like he was betraying Bryce. *We're not accusing him of cheating,* Justin reminded himself. *We're just trying to figure out if* someone *is cheating.* "I've got an idea."

CHAPTER 6

"You're sure no one's going to catch us in here?" Katie asked. Justin had led her to the baseball team's equipment room next to the gym.

"The team is out practicing, and they just started, so we should have plenty of time."

They stepped inside the tiny room and closed the door behind them. The room was a mess. Gloves, crates of balls, and old jerseys were thrown around with barely any organization. The room desperately needed to be cleaned too. Looking around, Justin wondered how they were going to find anything in this chaos.

"It smells like an entire gym threw up in here," Katie said, covering her mouth and nose with her hand.

"We won't have to be in here very long. It's not that big of a room."

Justin didn't know where to start. He opened a locker and glanced inside, but it was empty except for a stack of papers on top of some old cleats that looked like they hadn't been worn in years.

"Wouldn't the bats be out with the team while they practice?" Katie asked.

"No," Justin replied, sifting through the papers in the locker. "Remember? Bryce told us they use different bats for practice. They want to keep the equipment they use for games in ideal condition. So the game bats should be in here somewhere . . ."

He trailed off. He was looking at a piece of paper that read:

F—1: Hat, Ear, Nose

CU—2: Ear, Nose, Hat

S—3: Nose, Ear, Hat

CH—4: Hat, Ear, Hat . . .

And it went on from there.

"What are you looking at?" Katie jolted him out of his train of thought.

"I think it's the coach's signs." He pointed at the *F*. "See, if Coach Savino wants the pitcher to throw a fastball, this'll be his signal to the catcher: touching his hat, then his ear, and then his nose." He skimmed down the list. "If he wants a player to try to steal a base, he'll cough? That's weird."

Katie took the stack of papers out of Justin's hand. "Why are there multiple copies of this key? It looks like they're all different."

"I don't know—maybe different signs for each game? That would lower the chances of the other team figuring out the signs." And it might explain why these signs were so blatant compared to the subtle signals Justin had seen the coach use during the last few games. "Seems a little paranoid, though."

"Let's keep looking for the bats," Katie said. There weren't any bats lying around in the room. There were five lockers against one of the walls, and looking at them, Justin noticed that only the one on the far right had a padlock on it. He walked over and tapped the side of the locker. Inside they heard wood rolling around and knocking together. "Sounds like they're in there."

"Interesting that they're locked up," Katie said, crossing her arms.

Justin nodded, staring at the locker.

Then Katie stepped toward the door, where a clipboard was hanging on the wall. She pulled it off its hook and started glancing through the pages. "Hey, look at this. It's an equipment checkout list." Justin came over to where she was standing. She pointed to one of the first entries. "Someone checked out the bats a couple of days before the first game, but they didn't leave a name."

She looked up at Justin. "Who do you think has the combo for the padlock?"

"Coach Savino for sure—maybe some of the players too?"

"I suppose we can't really ask Bryce, can we?"

Just then, the door swung open, whacking

Katie in the back. Bryce poked his head around it. "Guys? What are you doing in here?"

"We—uhh—we were just—" Justin stammered.

"Why aren't you at practice?" Katie blurted out, which wasn't much better.

Bryce stepped into the room and closed the door just enough so they couldn't slip by him if they tried to run—not that they were going to. "I came in to run to the restroom, and I heard your voices in here. But you haven't answered my question. What are you doing?" He paused for a moment. "You guys are checking to see if we're cheating, aren't you? I thought you let that go!"

"We did let it go!" said Katie. "We just, uh, thought we should also keep a leash on it, just to be on the safe side."

What? thought Justin. He had no idea where she was going with that metaphor.

"You think this is a joke?" Bryce burst out, his face flushed. "You're accusing my team of cheating!"

"We aren't accusing you—" Justin started.

Bryce cut him off. "No, don't bother explaining. You really are a piece of work, Justin. You can't play on the team yourself, so you'll do anything to feel like you're part of the action."

"What? What's that supposed to mean?"

"You heard me. You're desperate to get Coach Savino's attention. To feel like you actually matter, like you're not just some sad kid whose dreams will never come true."

Justin saw Katie's mouth drop open in shock. But he was pretty sure he didn't react at all. Bryce's accusation paralyzed him. *Is that really what Bryce thinks of me? Does he really believe I'd imagine a cheating scandal just to make myself feel closer to the team?*

Bryce let the words hang in the air for a second before he turned around and left, slamming the door behind him. Justin and Katie were left in the silent room.

CHAPTER 7

"How long do you think Bryce is going to be mad?" Katie asked at lunch on Monday.

"I'll be kind of surprised if he ever talks to us again," Justin said. "He never answered my texts this weekend."

Katie shook her head and took a bite out of her burger. "Apology texts never work. And anyway, he owes *you* an apology after what he said to you. That was totally out of line."

"I mean—it wasn't true, but I understand why he said it." Justin stared down at his untouched lunch tray. "I'm thinking of skipping the game tomorrow."

Katie gave him a sad look. "We could still go. We don't have to talk to him afterward. We could just leave."

"I think that's even more pathetic than not going in the first place."

"Hey, guys." Justin looked up. Bryce was standing next to their table, holding his tray and looking nervous. "Um. Mind if I join you?" Both Katie and Justin gestured to the open seat. He sat down. "Look, I'm sorry about yesterday. I shouldn't have yelled at you guys. And Justin, I—I didn't mean any of that."

"I know you didn't," Justin said. "Don't worry about it. And we shouldn't have gone behind your back. We promise that we won't do that again."

Bryce put a hand up. "Actually, I'm glad you didn't let go of the whole cheating thing. I was mad at first, but during practice, I thought about it some more, and I think you guys have a point."

Katie set down her burger and sat up straight. "Just so we're clear," she said, "you think the team is cheating too?"

He nodded. "A couple of players, not the whole team, but yeah."

"What changed your mind?" asked Justin.

"I was watching us play, and—well— it was a lot like last year. I mean, we're definitely better, but we weren't batting very well and—I don't know. It just wasn't the same as a game."

"What's different?" Justin had a feeling he already knew, but he wanted to hear Bryce's firsthand impressions.

"We haven't hit a single home run in practice, not one. Even Derrick has trouble getting the ball deep into the outfield, and Coach has been telling him to hit as hard as he can."

Justin cocked an eyebrow at Katie. "This definitely supports your theory that someone messed with the game bats."

Bryce winced. "I guess that would explain why our hits are dramatically weaker when we're using practice bats . . . But I'm not sure it explains *everything*."

"Go on," said Katie.

"Well, it's not just the power of the hits that's different. It's how often we actually hit the ball in the first place. In practice we hit *maybe* sixty percent of the balls that we would in games. That has nothing to do with the bats we're using. It's specifically three guys too. Derrick is one. Bradley and Doug are the others."

Justin recalled all three of those players hitting balls deep into the outfield during the last two games. "Stealing signs," Justin murmured. He hadn't meant to say it out loud. The thought just occurred to him and popped out of his mouth.

"What?" Katie said.

"Stealing signs," Bryce echoed, his voice grim. "That's when players know the signs for what a pitcher will throw. You're not supposed to do it, but it happens. Players can pick up on what the opposing coach is signing to his own players, and they'll know what's coming next— what type of pitch, or if a player's about to steal a base. That kind of thing. It's one thing if the signs are really obvious, like Coach Bartlett's were. A five-year-old could've figured those out after a couple innings. But it's different if a team is going to a ton of trouble to steal signs."

"That sounds really hard to prove," Katie said.

"It is," Justin replied. "If the team's cheating in that way, we need concrete evidence. We need something we can expose."

"I wonder if that was what Matt was watching for," murmured Katie. When Bryce shot her a confused look, she explained, "We're not the only ones who are looking for cheating on the team. Matt's trying to find proof of it too."

"And we think he's planning to turn the cheaters in to Coach Savino," Justin added.

"So Matt's trying to get more people thrown off the team," Bryce said.

"Petty little guy, isn't he?" said Justin.

Bryce shook his head. "If someone is cheating, I don't want Matt to be the one who uncovers it. He doesn't deserve that satisfaction. Did you two find anything suspicious in the equipment room?"

"Not really," Justin said. "But the bats were locked up. We didn't get to take a look at them."

"I'll check them out tomorrow before the game," Bryce said. "I should have a chance to get into the equipment room while everyone's getting ready to play."

"And we'll keep an eye on the other players during the game," Justin said. "We'll see if anybody's paying a lot of attention to the other team's coach while he's sending signals."

Katie and Bryce nodded once again. "All right, let's do this."

CHAPTER 8

After two significant victories, more fans were coming out to see the Lions play. The third game of the season brought out twice as many fans as the first two combined. The bleachers were packed. Justin and Katie had to sit snugly between some other fans in the back row.

"There's our buddy," said Justin dryly, looking down and to the right. He'd spotted Matt right away.

"Give him a break," said Katie a little irritably. "He's not that different from you. You both love this team and can't be on it. Bryce kind of did have a point about that, even if he shouldn't have said what he said to you."

It hurt a little, but Justin knew that Katie was right. He and Matt were more similar than he'd wanted to admit. Neither of them could play, and they'd both reacted by operating behind the scenes—going behind the players' backs.

Justin scanned the players, looking for Bryce. He was warming up as usual. *Has he already looked at the bats?* Justin thought. He looked for Coach Savino and found him hanging on the dugout's chain-link fence, talking to Bradley, the second baseman, and Doug, the third baseman. *I wonder if he knows they might be cheating.*

The first two innings were fairly boring. Nobody scored, and only a handful of players got on base. At the top of the third, the opposing team's batter nailed one deep into center field. He got on first with time to spare. The second batter stepped up to the plate. After two balls, there was a sudden commotion. The player on first was stealing second base. He just barely made it. *It's a little early in the game to be stealing bases,* Justin thought. *Maybe we've got a reputation for winning this season, and they're trying to play aggressively right out of the gate.*

The other team didn't score. There were three outs before the player on second could get to third. Derrick stepped up to bat for the bottom of the third inning. The first pitch shot over the plate.

"Strike!"

Derrick moved his head around like he was cracking his neck. He glanced over at Coach Savino as the pitcher accepted the catcher's sign. Derrick got into the ready stance. The second pitch came and—*CRACK*—Derrick hit his third home run of the season. The crowd gave him a standing ovation as he ran around and jumped, planting both feet on home plate, clearly taunting the catcher.

"No way," Justin muttered. "No one's that good. He definitely knew what kind of pitch was coming his way."

"But that didn't seem to be true in the last two innings," Katie remarked. "So the players couldn't have known the signs ahead of time. And nobody on our team seems to be paying any attention to the other coach when he's signaling his players."

Justin's eyes drifted away from the field. "Wait a minute. What's Matt doing?"

"Uh, watching the game."

"Is he always that twitchy?"

"In general? No. But at games, yeah, I've noticed he fidgets a lot. Maybe he's getting frustrated he's not seeing any obvious cheating."

In the next inning, the opposing team once again managed to get a player on base. "I wonder if he's going to try to steal again," Katie remarked. He did, but this time, the runner wasn't nearly as successful. He'd barely made it off the base when the Lions pitcher, Kyle, pivoted and threw the ball to first. The runner hadn't even made it a third of the way before the first baseman tagged him out.

"Kyle has some suspiciously fast reflexes," Katie observed.

"Yeah," Justin said. "And he was looking at Coach Savino right before he nailed that guy. Savino must've signaled him."

"So Savino figured out the sign that the other coach was using?"

"I guess. But Savino hasn't looked toward the other coach this whole time. I don't get it. How can he figure out the signs if he's not watching the other coach like a hawk?"

The game was a slaughter. The Lions won ten to zero. The crowd stood up and applauded as the players came in from the outfield victorious. Justin was just able to catch sight of Matt packing up his things and heading straight for the Lions' dugout.

"Looks like Matt saw something interesting during the game," Justin said, pointing to him. "He's heading over to talk to Coach Savino."

They stayed in the stands watching him. He walked straight up to the coach, standing only a few feet from where all the players were gathered in a huddle celebrating. They talked for a moment. Matt had a serious look on his face—the look of someone asking for a big favor. Coach Savino shook his head, a response Matt clearly didn't want. He gestured toward the field and seemed to lose his cool a little bit. The coach shook his head again and turned away. Matt stared at the coach's back for a moment, looked at the ground, and slowly made his way toward the parking lot.

"Come on," Justin said. "Let's get down there."

The players were still congratulating each other on the victory when Justin and Katie walked up to the fence. Bryce was right in the middle of the crowd, patting people on the back. No one would ever guess that Bryce was suspicious of his teammates. He was celebrating just like he always would after a win. He wasn't acting strange at all—that was good.

Once the team dispersed a little, Bryce came up to them.

"Good game," Justin said.

"Not so much," Bryce said quietly.

"We're missing a bat!" Coach Savino was shouting over the murmur of the players gathering their things. "Where's the last bat?" He looked at Bryce, then at Katie and Justin.

Bryce put his hands up in an I-don't-know positon. The coach tapped some other players on the back. "Go find the last bat," he told them and walked away.

Once he was out of earshot, Bryce whispered to his friends, "I've got the bat. It's in my bag."

"Is there something up with it?" Justin asked.

Bryce immediately nodded. "Meet me at my house tonight. I've got to get my stuff." He walked away, high-fiving another player as if everything was fine.

"I'm going to talk to Coach Savino before we go," Justin told Katie. She said she'd wait in the car.

"You seen a bat lying around here?" The coach was on his knees looking under a bench. "I can't figure out where it went off to."

"No, I haven't seen it." *Not technically a lie*, Justin told himself. He hadn't actually seen the bat Bryce stole. "I did see Matt talking to you just now."

The coach looked straight at him. "Okay. And?"

"I—uh—I was just wondering if he's getting back on the team."

Coach Savino rolled his eyes. "Look, I'm sure you're aware that Matt was kicked off the team last year for cheating on a test."

Justin kept his expression neutral. No need for him to tell Savino that, in fact, he hadn't known why Matt was kicked off.

"The administration banned him from playing for the rest of his time here," the coach went on. "And anyway, I have a strong team now. We don't need him. But he's trying to get back in the good graces of the players. Keeping track of which players are out of position, strengths and weaknesses of opposing players, that kind of thing. So that the next time we play that team, we might be able to use that to our advantage."

"Is that really ethical—to have someone in the stands monitoring the other team during a game?"

The coach shrugged. "He doesn't tell me anything that I didn't already notice myself. It's harmless. Now if you want to make yourself useful, look around for that bat." He started searching again. It was clear that the discussion was over.

Justin headed to the parking lot, where Katie was still waiting in the idling car.

"What did the fearless leader have to say?" Katie said as Justin got in.

"He *really* wants to find that bat."

CHAPTER 9

Katie and Justin were playing table tennis in Bryce's garage when he got home.

"Your mom let us in," Justin explained. "We told her we were waiting for you."

"Hey," Katie said to Justin, "pick up your paddle. This is game point." After a quick volley, Katie won. "Ha, take that," she gloated.

Bryce put his sports bag off to the side and knelt down to unzip it. He pulled out the bat he had taken from the game and tossed it to Justin. "What do you think?"

Justin held the bat and examined it for a moment. "It seems okay to me. What's wrong with it?" Bryce grabbed another wooden bat, one of his own, from the corner of the garage. He handed it to Justin. The second bat was heavier—significantly heavier.

"Let me guess," Katie said, putting her table tennis paddle on the table. "They don't weigh the same, like they're supposed to." She held out her hand, and Justin passed her the lighter bat.

"Yup—it's been corked. Look, you can see it." Near the top of the bat, the grooves and lines of the wood abruptly cut off and changed into a circle. "Whoever did it didn't put the top back on exactly like it was." She pointed to the line where the grooves changed. "This is where it was cut open, and I'd bet every dollar I've got that it's filled with something other than wood."

"Let's find out," Bryce suggested. He went to another corner of the garage and produced a saw from inside a tool chest. Justin held the bat on the table while Katie sawed the top off exactly where it looked like it had been cut before. When she got all the way through, the top of the bat fell to the floor, and Katie turned it right-side up.

It was obvious. Someone had drilled out the

middle of the bat and packed cork in as tight as it would go.

Bryce used his finger to dig out a big chunk of the material. "So Derrick has been corking the bats."

Justin's forehead wrinkled. "If it was Derrick, don't you think he'd be a little more modest about his success? Less inclined to draw attention to himself?"

Bryce shrugged. "He might not be able to help himself. He's a pretty arrogant guy."

"But does he have the skills to cork a bat?" Katie asked. "Aside from the top being glued on incorrectly, this is some pretty advanced work. I don't think it was Derrick."

"So who do you think it was?" Bryce asked.

Justin looked at both of his friends. "Who do we know who has a talent in baseball *and* woodshop?"

/////

"Matt." Justin and Katie found him at his usual table in the library. They sat down across from him as he looked up from his work.

"Yeah?" Matt said coldly, as if they were interrupting something important.

"We'd like to talk to you about the bats that the baseball team is using."

Matt's face betrayed everything. His eyes started darting back and forth as if he were looking for an escape route. In a voice that was clearly straining to sound calm, he said, "What about them?"

"We got the chance to look at one of them. Turns out, someone corked it. You know anything about that?" Justin didn't take his eyes off Matt.

"I don't—I mean it wasn't—I don't—it could be anyone, right?"

Justin nodded. *Anyone, or just you*, he thought. "That's a good point. How about I take the bat to Coach Savino, and we let him figure it out?"

A bitter smirk flashed across Matt's face. "Sure, good luck with that."

"I have a better idea," said Katie. "We take it to an umpire during a game. Or, best idea yet, we take it to the principal."

Matt quickly put a hand on the table. "No, don't do that!" A student peeked out from behind one of the bookshelves and gave Matt a disapproving glance for the noise. "Don't do that," he said again, quieter this time.

"You corked the bats," Justin said.

"Yeah, I did, but it wasn't my idea." Matt was breathing a little heavier now.

"Really? So whose idea was it?"

Matt looked around to make sure no one was listening. "Coach Savino promised that if I helped him out, I could get back on the team. I went to him during tryouts and begged for a second chance. All I did was cheat on one test! And I only cheated because I was afraid of failing the class and getting kicked off the team."

"Pretty ironic that you got banned from playing anyway," said Justin. Katie shot him a look that made it clear he wasn't helping.

"Coach Savino said he understood where I was coming from. Said he'd talk to the administration. Said he'd get them to let me rejoin the team—as long as I did him a few favors first. But he lied. Last night after the game I asked him when I can start playing again. He said he didn't think there was an opening for me. I did all of it for nothing."

"What exactly do you mean by 'all of it'?" Katie asked.

"I'm not going to tell you, but I *will* tell you that the corking isn't the only thing that's going on."

With that, Matt took off as fast as he could from the library.

Katie turned to Justin. "I know I probably shouldn't, but I feel kind of bad for him."

"Nobody forced him to cheat," Justin reminded her. "And that goes for *both* times he's been involved in cheating at something. What he did put the whole team in jeopardy."

"I know, I know," she said, staring off into space. "But it was Savino who opened the door for him to do that. Savino took advantage of him—lied to him."

Justin couldn't argue with that. Of course Matt was responsible for his own choices, but Savino was the authority figure who'd made him believe those choices would pay off.

Katie sighed and seemed to shake off her thoughts. "So . . . what now?"

"Now I'm going to talk to Derrick."

"What makes you think he's going to confess anything?"

"Because the guy may be good at what he does, but he knows so little about baseball, he might not even know he's cheating."

/////

Justin caught up with Derrick just as he was on his way to practice. "Hey, mind if I talk to you for a second?" By this point, he knew who the real cheater on the team was. He just needed confirmation.

"I've got to get to practice," Derrick said dismissively. "What do you want?"

"I just wanted to say that I really admire your skill with a bat." *I'll appeal to his own inflated sense of self,* Justin thought. "The power of your hits aside, you've got some real reflexes there."

Derrick nodded approvingly at the comment. "It's a real talent."

"Yeah," Justin said. "It's like you know what the pitcher's going to throw before he even does it."

Now Derrick looked a little confused. "Well . . . yeah," he said. "Of course I do."

"Really? How?"

"Coach tells me." Derrick said it like it was knowledge any baseball fan would have. "When the pitcher's getting ready, I look at Coach and he gives me a sign telling me whether it's going to be a fastball, a curveball, or whatever else the guy's going to throw."

"He gives you a sign?"

"Yeah. Why?"

Justin pinched his nose between his eyes. This guy really was kind of clueless. "Derrick, has it ever occurred to you that Coach isn't supposed to know what the pitcher's going to throw?"

Derrick looked confused and maybe a little offended. "It's an insider thing, something Coach learned how to do when he was in the minor leagues. Coach said that he thought

Bradley, Doug, and I were good enough to do it. We're not supposed to tell the other players, because he didn't want them to be offended. And other teams don't do it because their players aren't smart enough to pull it off."

"That's not why they don't do it," Justin said, trying to keep his voice even. "It's against the rules for players—or a coach—to steal another coach's signs."

Derrick shook his head, clearly unconvinced. "Well, Coach says all really good teams do it. And it's not like there's a law or something."

/////

"It's Coach Savino," Justin said to Bryce at the pizza place after Bryce finished practice. "He's the one who told Matt to cork the bats, and he's been having Matt steal the other teams' signs. That's why Matt was watching the games. He was keeping an eye on the other team's coach."

Katie added, "It always took him a few innings to figure out the meanings of the signs, which is why the early parts of the games were normal. Then Matt would start passing the other coach's signs to Savino, and Savino would signal his players."

"He never did that for me," Bryce said quickly.

"It was only Derrick, Bradley, and Doug. Derrick confirmed that when I talked to him."

"What about Kyle?" asked Katie. "He's got to be in on it too, right? Remember in the last game, when that opposing player tried to steal a base, and Savino signaled Kyle to get him?"

"Derrick didn't say anything about Kyle being involved. It's possible that Kyle just thinks Savino has a good eye and good instincts. And I can't speak for Bradley and Doug, but Derrick didn't even know he was cheating. In fact, he still didn't believe me when I tried to explain it to him."

Bryce groaned and rested his face in his hands. "What a mess."

"There's more," Katie added. "After every game, Matt would text the other team's signs to Savino—like, decoding them for him. That way Savino could keep lists of the other teams' signs for when the Lions played those teams again, later in the season."

"All of which is definitely against the rules," concluded Justin. "It's one thing for a coach or a player to pick up on another team's signs during a game. It's a whole other thing for someone in the stands to actively help out. And using that knowledge in the next game is way out of line."

Bryce sat up straight again, shaking his head. He looked as disappointed as Justin had ever seen him. "I really thought we had a chance at state this year."

"So what do we do?" Katie asked. "We can't just confront him about it. As soon as he knows we've caught on, he'll replace all the bats and stop stealing signs—or worse, find a more clever way to do it."

"We can report this to the umpires at the next game," Bryce suggested. "If we bring a corked bat to show them, that should be enough proof, right?"

"We'll need proof of the sign-stealing too," said Justin. "And proof that Coach Savino masterminded all of it. Otherwise he could just pretend Matt was acting alone when he corked the bats. And even if we get Matt and Derrick to talk, it'd be their word against Coach Savino's. He could claim that he never stole signs and that everyone else is lying about him."

"Yeah," sighed Katie. "Somehow I don't think a known cheater like Matt and a . . . non-genius like Derrick will win anybody's trust."

"So we have to find some other way to prove Coach's involvement," said Bryce.

Justin thought for a second. "The cheating needs to be really obvious during a game—obvious enough that the umpires can't miss it."

"Who are we playing next?"

Bryce said, "The Spartans, but we're playing at their field this time."

"That was the team we played first, right?"

"Yeah."

"Perfect," Justin said. "That means Matt already knows their signs. He can start feeding them to Savino right away. Savino won't even have to wait a few innings before he starts cheating."

"So what do we do?" Katie asked again.

Justin looked at them both and smiled. "We send an email."

CHAPTER 10

There was some preparation. Justin checked the Spartans' school website and found the email address for their baseball coach. Then he created a fake address—anonymousLion—and sent a message.

"I'm a student at Mason Falls High School. I've discovered that our baseball team, the Lions, has been cheating during the last few games. There are two ways they are doing this, and we would like to expose both of them during the next game, this Thursday, against your team. I can handle exposing one of the methods, but I'm going to need your help to expose the other."

It took several email exchanges to convince the coach that he was legit—and that his plan was the best way to deal with the situation. But eventually the coach agreed to help. Bryce took care of another part of the plan. He put the stolen bat back into the equipment room, but not before Katie had reassembled it . . . with some further alterations.

The last piece of the puzzle was Matt.

Justin found him in the hallway between periods.

"I'm not doing it," Matt said as soon as Justin explained his plan.

"It's nothing you haven't done before."

"I don't care," Matt said. "I'm done with the whole thing. I'm not even going to the Spartans game."

"Look, I'm glad you're ready to stop helping Savino. But we need to show everyone what he's been doing."

"And what happens when you do?" Matt burst out. "What do you think happens to me? He already lied about putting me back on the roster. He'll get me expelled for this."

Matt had a point, but Justin was ready with his answer. "If you help us expose Savino, he won't be able to talk his way out of it by pinning everything on you. And we'll make sure the administration knows you were working with us to uncover what he was doing. It's like when people who get arrested cut deals, you know? You've switched over to the right side, so we won't let Savino drag you down with him."

Matt bit his bottom lip and eyed Justin doubtfully. At last he gave a little nod. Justin knew he'd help.

As Justin followed Katie to the Spartans' field, he was both excited and a little terrified. He had no idea how Savino would react once the cheating was exposed, and the last thing he wanted was for the coach to take it out on Bryce.

"You don't think this is a little . . ." Katie waved her hand around, searching for a word. "Excessive? Dramatic?"

Justin shrugged. "Maybe, but it's our best shot. It won't give Savino any time to hide the evidence of what he's been doing. And anyway, it's a little late to back out now."

Katie huffed a little laugh. "Should be an interesting game."

Once again, the stands were full of fans expecting to see another Lions win. *They have no idea what's about to happen*, Justin thought as he passed fellow students dressed in the school colors, some even holding signs. Toward the top of the bleachers, Justin caught the eye of Matt, who chose to fiddle with his phone instead of acknowledge Justin.

Justin was on edge. He watched the players warm up and tried to act as if everything were normal, but he found himself restless. He couldn't concentrate on anything. One of the players picked up a bat to practice his swing, and Justin watched him give the bat a puzzled look, but the player shrugged it off and started swinging at the air in front of him.

"That could have been it right there," Katie muttered to Justin. "What if that player had taken the bat to an umpire? The cheating would've been exposed before the game even started."

"Or he could have taken it to Coach Savino, and it could have been covered up again," Justin pointed out.

As if on cue, Savino looked up from the dugout, and his gaze locked on Justin's face. *He knows*, Justin's paranoid brain screamed. *He knows, and he's going to find a way to pin this all on me.*

The coach looked away, and Justin's eyes darted from player to player as his mind raced. *If Coach Savino found out what we did to the bat, he'll know for sure that someone figured it out. I've talked to him after every game. He'd probably—*

"Would you calm down?" Katie startled him out of his train of thought. "You look like we're about to steal the Mona Lisa."

"Right," Justin said, taking a deep breath and trying to control his thoughts. *We need to expose the bat tampering and the sign stealing. Then there'll be no way that Savino can pretend he wasn't involved. Every part of the plan has to go exactly right.*

The game was about to start. He glanced at the Spartans' coach. *I hope he follows through with his part of the plan*, Justin thought. It was impossible to tell what the coach was thinking. He paced from one end of the dugout to the other, looking calm and focused—business as usual.

Derrick stepped up to bat, and Justin sucked in some air as he tapped the bat on home plate. *This is it.* He saw the opposing coach lean closer as if he were paying special attention to what was about to happen.

The first pitch came. "Ball!" the umpire shouted. The second pitch—"Strike!" Derrick had swung powerfully, but failed to connect. The third pitch—*CRACK*—the ball sailed high over center field, but a Spartan outfielder caught it just short of the fence. Derrick was out.

Justin watched the bat as Derrick tossed it toward their team's dugout. *Must not have been that one.*

Bradley, another cheater, stepped up to the plate. Justin knew him by his number. The whole process seemed to unfold in slow motion. The Spartans pitcher leaned in, squinting at the catcher. Matt watched the Spartans coach and quickly made a motion. The pitcher nodded, accepting the sign. For a brief moment, Justin saw Bradley glance at Coach Savino, who made the same motion. The pitch came.

This time, the sound was a crack, combined with a crunch. *That's the one*, Justin thought. The bat exploded into about a dozen splintered pieces. The spectators surged to their feet, excited by the apparent power of the hit. It had been a line drive toward left field, and Bradley easily got to first, but Justin wasn't watching him.

The umpire was collecting the pieces of the broken bat, staring hard at the broken wood. The crowd was still wildly applauding when the umpire's screeching whistle pierced through the noise. He gestured for both coaches to join him at home plate and waved the players away.

The two coaches and the umpire stood at the plate speaking for a while. The umpire was clearly showing them something on the broken piece of wood.

"So I'm guessing the umpire knows that bat was completely hollow," Katie said quietly to Justin. "Do you think he'll be able to tell there was cork in it at some point?"

"I'm sure we missed some flakes of it when we were digging it out," Justin replied. "And they'll definitely weigh the other bats and realize something's off."

Savino gestured to one of the players. The player gathered the Lions' wooden bats and brought them over to the plate. The umpire picked up each one, testing the weight in his hand. Savino spread his palms in a gesture that seemed to say "I had no idea." He kept his expression innocent as he spoke to the umpire. *Probably trying to pin it on Matt*, Justin thought grimly.

The opposing coach was clearly not happy. While Coach Savino strolled to the Lions' dugout, his competitor stormed off to his. Bradley was called out, and the crowd gave a chorus of "Booooo!" Meanwhile, the Spartans coach spoke to one of his players, who ran over to the Lions' dugout carrying three of their metal bats. The next Lions batter used one of these.

A couple of their players made it onto base, but they didn't get any runs. The score was still zero to zero at the bottom of the first inning.

The Spartans were up again. The first pitch came, and the batter nailed it: a grounder too fast for Bryce to snag before it bounced into left field. The player made it to first with time to spare.

This was it. Justin's eyes darted back and forth between the player and the Spartans coach.

During the first two pitches to the next batter, the player stayed planted firmly on first base. But then Justin saw the Spartans coach give him a signal. Justin glanced at Matt, who was already giving a signal to Savino, which a moment later was relayed to the pitcher. Kyle wound up, but instead of throwing it over the plate, he wheeled around and threw the ball full speed to the first baseman. The player had never moved a muscle.

There was a moment of confusion in the crowd. Everyone knew they'd just seen something strange. There was no clear reason for Kyle to have made that throw, when the player was clearly still on his base. The Spartans coach came running out of their dugout shouting, "Time out!" at the top of his lungs.

Once again, the umpire waved away the players as both coaches approached home plate. This time, the Spartans coach was furious, yelling and pointing at Savino. Justin and Katie were too far away to hear exactly what was going on, but it was pretty clear: Savino was being accused of stealing signs, and the Spartans had just exposed it. The Spartans coach had given a pre-arranged fake-out sign to his player on first base. That sign—a cue for the player to steal second base—had caused a revealing chain reaction. Kyle had thrown the ball to second, expecting a steal attempt that clearly wasn't happening. Sign stealing was the only explanation for why he would've done that.

The umpire asked Savino some questions. Justin could see the coach shaking his head and holding up his hands in protest. The Spartans coach was furious, shouting and pointing a finger harshly at Savino. The Lions coach stepped closer to the umpire and whispered something. When Justin saw the ump shaking his head no, he knew that whatever Savino had just tried hadn't worked. Before long, the umpire turned around and addressed the crowd.

"The Lions forfeit!"

There wasn't any applause, even from the other team. Instead, there was a general murmur of confusion and questions. A Mason Falls student stood up and shouted "Why?" but both coaches and the umpire pretended not to hear.

Justin and Katie looked from the umpire to Bryce. Their friend was standing between second and third base, looking down and shaking his head. Justin glanced over to where Matt had been sitting, but he was already gone.

CHAPTER 11

The next day at school, Justin still had trouble focusing on anything besides the Lions.

"Coach resigned," Bryce reported at the end of the day when the three friends met up at Katie's locker. "And Derrick and the other guys were suspended from the team too."

"How's the rest of the team taking it?"

Bryce shrugged and opened a bag of chips. "Everybody's kind of shocked. But I don't want to win state by cheating, and most of the guys feel the same way."

"So Savino's gone?" Justin asked.

"Not yet," Katie said unexpectedly as she closed her locker door. "I spotted him earlier today. He's probably cleaning out his office."

Justin looked down the hall toward the gymnasium. "I want to talk to him."

"Why?" Bryce stuffed some chips into his mouth.

"I just want to know why he did it."

"Be my guest. You know where to go."

/////

The door to the coach's office was open. Inside, Savino was emptying the contents of a shelf into a cardboard box.

The former coach glanced over his shoulder and seemed to recognize him but then quickly looked back at the box. "What do you want?" he said.

"I'm just curious why you did it."

Savino dropped a plaque into the box. "I was trying to help."

"By cheating?"

"By boosting the team's standing," he replied. "I wasn't just helping the players who knew what was going on. I was helping the whole group." He didn't look at Justin while he spoke, just stared at the wall as if there were a window there instead of empty shelves. "They were all going to be good players on a good team. That earns college acceptance letters and scholarships."

"And what would have happened when Derrick went off to college and his batting average took a dramatic drop?" Justin asked.

After a beat of silence, Savino said, "Doesn't matter now."

"It matters to the guys who got suspended for cheating," Justin said quietly. "And the other players who trusted you and got let down. It matters to Matt, whom you manipulated into helping you. And it matters to all the fans of the team. It matters a lot. Just not to you, I guess." He walked away without waiting for a response.

/////

With the team "in transition," the Lions forfeited their next three games. The teams they would have played were credited with victories even though those games never happened.

Meanwhile Mr. Yang, one of the social studies teachers, took over as the new coach, and the team held vigorous practices. On the plus side, the school sprang for metal bats. They didn't want to be accused of cheating again.

"He's working us hard," Bryce told his friends. "But we're improving as a team."

"Not as dramatically this time, I hope?" said Katie wryly.

"Nah." Bryce smiled. "We're improving at a rate that actually makes sense."

Eventually the Lions were scheduled to actually play a game. Justin was excited for it, especially because this time he wouldn't have to look for suspicious activity. He was on his way between classes when Mr. Yang stopped him.

"You're Justin, right?" the man said.

"Yeah." Justin had never had him for class, so he wasn't sure why Mr. Yang recognized him.

"I just started coaching the baseball team a few weeks ago, and I've been talking with your friend Bryce. He tells me you're a big baseball fan. Can't play though?"

"Yeah," Justin said, pointing to his left knee. "Knee trouble."

"Well, Bryce also told me what you did for the team. It got me thinking—I could really use an assistant coach. You know, another pair of eyes on the players. Is that something you'd be interested in?"

Justin felt his eyes go wide. He hadn't realized this was even a possibility. If he had, he would have tried to do it years ago. "Absolutely!"

Mr. Yang gave a little chuckle. "Great! You'll start tomorrow. Practice is right after school. I'll make sure they get you a shirt and a hat. See you soon."

"Thank you!" Justin stammered as the coach walked away. Mr. Yang gave a little wave over his shoulder and continued down the hall.

When Justin got to lunch, it was clear that Bryce already knew what had happened. He must have told Katie too, because they both congratulated him before he even said anything.

"I still feel bad about saying you were trying to live through me," Bryce said as Justin sat down. "I hope this helps a little."

Justin waved the apology away. "Water under the bridge. But thanks for putting in a good word for me."

"You're perfect for the job too. I don't think I've ever met anyone as committed to baseball as you."

"Here's to the new assistant coach," Katie said, raising a milk carton.

"To the Lions," Justin said. And then, out of habit, he added with a grin, "This could be the year we win state."

That night, Katie and Justin watched the Lions take the field once again. It was a close game, but in the end, the Lions lost five to four after two extra innings. When they went up to the fence to talk to Bryce, he shrugged off the loss. "At least we played honestly."

The score didn't bother Justin either. It was the last game he'd watch as a mere fan.

MASON FALLS MYSTERIES

BEHIND THE SCREEN
THE HOUSE
TRACKS
THE TURNAROUND

EVEN AN ORDINARY TOWN
HAS ITS SECRETS.

DAY OF DISASTER

Would you survive?

ABOUT THE AUTHOR

R. T. Martin lives in St. Paul, Minnesota. When he is not drinking coffee or writing, he is busy thinking about drinking coffee and writing.